Please help the bunnies of Moonglo

Our brave and loyal friend, ... our world to protect the magi... keeps our kingdom safe from the dark rabbits. Arrow is very far from home and will need your help.

Could you be his friend?

This magic bunny might be hard to spot as he is very small and often appears in different fluffy bunny disguises—but you can recognize him by the rainbow twinkle in his eyes.

Thank you for your help!

Strike
Leader of Moonglow Meadow

For Roger—so sleek and beautiful with coal-black fur—SB

GROSSET & DUNLAP
Published by the Penguin Group
Penguin Group (USA) Inc., 375 Hudson Street, New York, New York 10014, USA
Penguin Group (Canada), 90 Eglinton Avenue East, Suite 700, Toronto, Ontario M4P 2Y3, Canada
(a division of Pearson Penguin Canada Inc.)
Penguin Books Ltd., 80 Strand, London WC2R 0RL, England
Penguin Group Ireland, 25 St. Stephen's Green, Dublin 2, Ireland (a division of Penguin Books Ltd.)
Penguin Group (Australia), 250 Camberwell Road, Camberwell, Victoria 3124, Australia
(a division of Pearson Australia Group Pty. Ltd.)
Penguin Books India Pvt. Ltd., 11 Community Centre, Panchsheel Park, New Delhi—110 017, India
Penguin Group (NZ), 67 Apollo Drive, Rosedale, North Shore 0632, New Zealand
(a division of Pearson New Zealand Ltd.)
Penguin Books, Rosebank Office Park, 181 Jan Smuts Avenue, Parktown North 2193, South Africa
Penguin China, B7 Jaiming Center, 27 East Third Ring Road North,
Chaoyang District, Beijing 100020, China

Penguin Books Ltd., Registered Offices: 80 Strand, London WC2R 0RL, England

 First printed in Great Britain in 2010 by Puffin Books. First published in the United States in 2013 by Grosset & Dunlap, a division of Penguin Young Readers Group, 345 Hudson Street, New York, New York 10014. GROSSET & DUNLAP is a trademark of Penguin Group (USA) Inc. Printed in the U.S.A.

Library of Congress Cataloging-in-Publication Data is available.

ISBN 978-0-448-46727-6 10 9 8 7 6 5 4 3 2

ALWAYS LEARNING PEARSON

Chocolate Wishes

SUE BENTLEY

illustrated by Angela Swan

Grosset & Dunlap
An Imprint of Penguin Group (USA) Inc.

Prologue

Arrow glanced around Moonglow Meadow as he emerged from the burrow. A rainbow shone in his warm brown eyes. Lush grass waved gently in the night breeze, and the air was soft with the scent of wild flowers. Other magic rabbits were nibbling juicy leaves or hopping about in the moonlight.

Bending his head, Arrow began grooming his velvety white fur, which was flecked with silver. A tiny gold key he wore on a fine chain around his neck gave a bell-like tinkle. As the chosen keeper of the magical key, Arrow was responsible for looking after it.

A large older rabbit with a wise expression and a dark gray snout bounded toward him. Arrow saw that Strike looked tired and that there was dust in his fur.

"I did not expect you to return so soon." Arrow bowed in greeting before the leader of the warren. "When are the dark rabbits coming to live with us?"

Strike shook his head wearily. "They refused. The dark rabbits are unwilling to share our land."

"I do not understand." Arrow was puzzled. The deep gully next to Moonglow Meadow was home to a neighboring warren of dark rabbits. Their land had become so dry that nothing grew there anymore, and they were hungry. "How will they survive without our help?"

"By stealing what we treasure the most! Our magic key!" Strike rumbled, his face darkening. "They want to use it to make their gully green and beautiful again. They are not far behind me and are coming soon."

Arrow gasped and his tail twitched nervously. "But without the key's power, Moonglow Meadow will become a desert and we will starve. What can we do?"

Strike extended a muscular paw and rested it gently on Arrow's shoulder. "You must go to the Otherworld. Hide there with the key so the dark rabbits cannot find it."

Arrow gulped at the thought of all the unknown dangers. He felt very young and afraid, but he took a deep breath and then lifted his head. "I will do it."

Strike smiled with pride and affection. "There is no time to waste!" Lifting his head, he gave a soft but piercing cry.

Every rabbit in the warren pricked up its ears and came hurrying toward them. They formed a circle around Arrow. Suddenly, the golden key glowed so brightly that Arrow couldn't see a thing.

The light faded slowly and where the young white-and-silver magic rabbit had been now stood a tiny fluffy white bunny with huge golden-brown eyes that gleamed with tiny rainbows.

"Use this disguise," Strike ordered. "Only return when we need more of the key's magic to protect our meadow. And watch out for the dark rabbits! They will be looking for you."

Arrow straightened his small fluffy shoulders. "I will not fail the warren!"

Thud. Thud. Thud. The rabbits began thumping their feet in time. Arrow felt the magic building and a cloud of crystal dust sparkled around him as Moonglow Meadow began to fade . . .

Chapter ONE

Dawn Kenton's heart beat quickly as she opened the classroom door. She hoped her new teacher would find her someone friendly to sit next to. She was already missing her friends from her old school.

The teacher was taking attendance. Dawn hovered in the doorway, not sure whether she should knock politely or say something.

Oh, great. I'm late on my very first day at

my new school, she thought. She felt herself blushing as the whole class turned to look at her.

Just as Dawn was gathering her courage to speak, Miss Walker lifted her head and spotted her. She had short brown hair and glasses, and had seemed really nice when Dawn came to see the school with her mom and dad a few weeks ago.

The teacher came over. "Hello there. Come on in." She put an encouraging hand on Dawn's shoulder and led her into the classroom. "Listen up, class. This is Dawn Kenton; she just moved into the area. I want you all to make her feel welcome."

"Hi, Dawn," called a loud chorus of voices.

Dawn managed a shy grin.

Miss Walker pointed toward the back of the room. "There's a seat open next to Emma Packard. Emma will show you around, but remember to come and see me if you ever have any problems. Okay?"

"Thank you." Head down, Dawn scooted toward the empty chair.

Behind her, the teacher finished taking attendance.

Two girls nudged each other and giggled as Dawn walked past them. "Let's see what Emma does!" one of them whispered.

Dawn tried not to turn around and look at them, but she wondered what they meant. She sat down next to her new classmate and slid her schoolbag under the desk.

Emma made a face at the two girls who had whispered. She had short hair, blue eyes, and a pretty heart-shaped face. Turning back to Dawn, she shrugged. "Don't worry about Alesha and Vicky. They're just jealous because I get to make a new friend! You can put your stuff in this drawer," she said helpfully.

"Um . . . thanks," Dawn said gratefully, relieved that Emma seemed nice.

It wasn't just her old school friends that Dawn missed. She was still feeling strange after moving into the new apartment. Pets weren't allowed in Redford Mansions, so Tansy, Dawn's beloved Jack Russell, had gone to live with her aunt. Dawn knew it would be a long time before she stopped missing her little dog.

As she bent down and began searching through her bag, her light-brown shoulder-length hair swung forward. Dawn tucked a strand behind one ear and with her free hand pulled out a pile of books.

"Oh!" She gasped as the heavy books slid out of her grip and fell to the floor with a crash.

The kids sitting nearby almost jumped out of their seats.

"Sorry," Dawn murmured. She dropped to her knees to pick up the books.

Emma leaned over to help her, but Dawn was so flustered she didn't notice. She got up quickly and her head accidentally brushed against Emma's forehead.

"Ow!" Emma exclaimed loudly, clapping her hand over her eye. "You clumsy dummy! You almost knocked my eyes out!"

"Oh, gosh! Sorry . . ." Dawn chewed her lip. She didn't think it had been that bad, but Emma was making such a fuss that Dawn didn't dare say anything. "Maybe you need first aid or something. I'll go and tell Miss Walker."

As she stood up, Emma and the two girls in front burst into giggles.

Dawn looked blankly at them. Emma seemed to have recovered completely. What was going on?

"Got you!" Emma laughed, her eyes sparkling. "That was *too* easy!"

Dawn smiled awkwardly, trying to see the funny side.

"Is something wrong, dear?" Miss Walker called out.

"Um, no. I . . . I . . . I'm fine," Dawn stuttered, realizing that she was still standing up. As dozens of pairs of eyes turned to stare at her she felt herself

turning bright red and she wished the floor would open up and swallow her. To her horror, she felt her eyes prickling with tears and quickly sat down again.

"All right, class," the teacher clapped her hands. "Take out your workbooks please. With Easter approaching, we're studying different customs around the world."

"Hey, what's wrong?" Emma said, glancing sideways at Dawn.

Dawn blinked hard. She hated being made fun of and all of a sudden she missed her old life, her friends, and Tansy even more. But she didn't say any of that.

"I'm fine," she murmured again. "Just leave me alone."

Emma shrugged and bent over her workbook. "Suit yourself."

At lunchtime, Dawn found an empty table and sat by herself to eat her lunch. Emma was with a group of girls nearby. "Hey, Dawn! Come over here!" she called.

Dawn thought about going over, but they were all laughing loudly and joking around. She didn't want to be the butt of their jokes for a second time that day, so she hunched her shoulders and pretended she hadn't heard.

The rest of the day seemed to crawl by. When the final bell rang, Dawn escaped as quickly as she could.

She grabbed her coat from the coatroom and flew out of the school.

She swung her schoolbag by its long strap as she hurried home to the nearby apartment. She sighed heavily, thinking about how before Tansy would have run to her the moment she got in, her stubby tail twirling. School and home really weren't very happy places to be right now.

Dawn turned into the gardens that surrounded Redford Mansions. It seemed quiet in there and she could sit by herself until she felt less upset. Otherwise her mom would notice that she looked sad and start asking questions, and she didn't want to worry her.

She threw her bag on a bench and sat down next to it. Suddenly, there was a bright flash, and a shower of crystal dust drifted toward Dawn like a glimmering cloud.

Dawn screwed up her face, trying to make sense of what she was seeing. As the

dust slowly dissolved, she spotted a tiny fluffy white bunny on the grass.

"Can you help me please?" it asked in a scared little voice.

Chapter TWO

Dawn's eyes widened as she stared at the cute little bunny in complete astonishment before shaking her head for being silly. Talking animals only existed in fairy tales, not in real life!

The bunny's long floppy ears lifted, and it twitched its pink nose nervously. Dawn walked slowly forward and then hunched down so she wouldn't frighten it.

"Hello there," she said gently, reaching out her hand. "Aren't you adorable? I wonder how you got here. You can't belong to anyone in the building."

"That is true. I do not belong to anyone. I have just arrived," the bunny said in a shaky little voice.

Dawn did a double take and stopped herself, jerking her hand back as if she'd been burned. "You . . . You really can talk! How come?"

"All the rabbits in my world can talk," Arrow told her, lifting his little head proudly. "I am Arrow, guardian of Moonglow Meadow. May I know your name?"

"Um . . . sure. I'm Dawn. Dawn Kenton. I live in one of these apartments with my parents." For the first time she noticed that the bunny had gorgeous brown eyes that seemed to glimmer with tiny rainbows.

Arrow bowed his head. "I am honored to meet you, Dawn."

"Likewise." Dawn bowed awkwardly. "Where is Moonglow Meadow?" It sounded beautiful, but Dawn had never heard of such a place.

Arrow shook his head and something around his neck tinkled softly. Dawn saw that he wore a fine gold chain with a key hanging from it. "Moonglow Meadow is where my warren lives."

Dawn nodded. She knew that "warren" was the name used for a group of rabbits who all lived together. At her old school she'd done a project about animal groups. "I didn't know there were any meadows or fields near here. Is it far away?"

"Yes, very far. In another world," Arrow explained. "I am keeper of the magic key, which keeps our meadow lush and green. But our neighbors, who are fierce dark rabbits, are trying to steal it. Their land is dry and stony, and they will not share the meadow with us. They want to use the key's magic to change their own land. If they do this, Moonglow Meadow will become a desert."

"Oh no! That would be awful!" Dawn exclaimed.

"Yes, it would. That is why I was sent here to hide and keep the magic key safe."

Dawn nodded slowly, looking at the tiny bunny more closely. "I don't mean to be rude, but aren't you a bit small for such an important mission?"

Rainbows gleamed more brightly in Arrow's warm brown eyes. "Please stand clear," he ordered, rising up onto his back legs.

Dawn felt a strange warm tingling sensation down her spine as the key around his neck began flashing and a cloud of shimmering crystal dust swirled about Arrow. When it cleared, Dawn saw that the cute little bunny had vanished and in his place stood the most amazing and majestic rabbit she had ever seen. It was as big as a large cat and had silky white fur flecked with silver. The tips of its ears looked as if they'd been dipped in silver glitter, and its chocolate-brown eyes flashed with jewel-bright rainbows.

Dawn gasped. Nothing could have prepared her for such a magnificent sight.

"Arrow?" She gulped in wonderment.

"Yes, it is still me, Dawn," Arrow said in a smooth, velvety voice.

Before she had gotten used to seeing Arrow in his true form there was a final glow of light from his key and he appeared as a tiny fluffy white bunny again.

"Wow! That's an amazing disguise!"

Arrow twitched his white whiskers nervously. "I am afraid it will not fool the dark rabbits if any of them find me. I must hide quickly."

"You can stay with m—" Dawn began eagerly. "Oh, I keep forgetting that we're not allowed pets in our new apartment."

Arrow dipped his head in a shallow

bow. "I understand. I will ask another person to help me. Thank you for your kindness. It was nice to meet you, Dawn." He took two small hops toward a nearby bush.

"No! Please, wait!" Dawn burst out.

She couldn't bear to lose him, especially as no one else had been friendly to her all day. As a big, strong rabbit with thick white fur Arrow was magnificent as guardian of his meadow. But as a tiny fluffy bunny with melting brown eyes he was totally adorable and Dawn just wanted to help him.

She thought hard. "I know! I'll smuggle you into our apartment inside my schoolbag. Mom's going shopping straight after work and Dad won't be back until later, so no one will notice. You can stay in my bedroom with me."

Arrow's eyes twinkled gratefully. "Thank you, Dawn. I would like very much to stay with you."

Dawn opened her schoolbag and placed it on the ground. Arrow kicked up his back legs, leaped inside, and settled down next to her tiger-print pencil case.

"Let's go!" Dawn zipped the bag, leaving a small opening so he could

breathe. They went into Redford Mansions through the main doors. "We're on the third floor, so I usually use the elevator. It might feel a bit odd to you at first," she warned him.

"I am not afraid. I know that I will be safe with you," Arrow said in a muffled voice.

Dawn felt a surge of pride that the tiny little bunny trusted her. She was looking forward to taking care of Arrow and finding out more about him. It might even help her feel a bit less lonely for Tansy. Her heart felt lighter than it had for days.

Chapter THREE

"There. How's that?" Dawn tucked Arrow into the cozy nest she'd just made by tucking a wool scarf inside an old shoe box.

Arrow sniffed around, nibbling and pawing at the scarf before curling up with his nose between his fluffy white paws. "This is a good place to sleep."

Dawn smiled, delighted that he liked it. She picked up the box, ready to take it into her bedroom, when the kitchen door

banged open. Her mom stag
two shopping bags.

Dawn jumped guiltily. She had no chance to hide Arrow. "Mom! You're back!"

"Hi, honey!" Mrs. Kenton said cheerily. Crossing the room, she dumped the groceries on the counter. "I was quicker than I expected. They opened a new line just as I got to the check-out." She started unpacking groceries. "How was your first day at school?"

Dawn braced herself to be yelled at when her mom eventually spotted Arrow in the kitchen. From the corner of her eye she noticed that the key around Arrow's neck was glowing again. "It was . . . um, okay," she said vaguely.

Why hadn't Mom said anything about Arrow? It was almost as if she hadn't seen him.

"What's that you're clutching?" Mrs. Kenton nodded toward the shoe box as she put a carton of milk in the fridge. "Is it part of a class project?"

"Yeah! We're doing"—Dawn fought for an explanation—"Easter stuff. I'm going to work on it in my bedroom. See you later!" She shot out of the kitchen and hurried into her bedroom.

Once the door was closed, Dawn placed

Arrow's box on her bedside chest of drawers. "Phew! That was close. I thought I was toast back there. Why didn't Mom see you?"

Arrow's tail waggled cheekily. "I used my magic to make myself invisible. Now only you will be able to see me and hear me talking to you."

"What a great idea! It makes it easier to hide you from Mom and Dad. Is anyone else allowed to know?"

"No. My presence here must be kept secret," Arrow said, looking serious. "You can tell no one about me, Dawn."

Dawn felt disappointed. She had wondered if Emma would be nicer to her if she knew a magic bunny had chosen her for his friend. But she was prepared to keep Arrow's secret, if it would help keep him and his key safe from the fierce dark rabbits. She didn't want to lose her only friend here.

"Okay, then. Cross my heart," she promised.

"Thank you, Dawn."

Dawn stroked his velvety ears with the tips of her fingers. "Why does that key around your neck keep flashing?"

"It makes my magic stronger," he explained. "When its power is needed for Moonglow Meadow the key will glow continuously. And I will have to return." As he finished speaking, Arrow's whiskers quivered and he yawned sleepily.

Dawn would have liked to ask him more about his strange and wonderful world, but he had already closed his eyes

with a sigh. Almost at once soft little bunny snores rose from the box.

Dawn gently tucked the scarf around her fluffy new friend. She'd only known Arrow for a short time, but she already loved him to pieces.

Dawn heard her dad come home from work, so she left Arrow snoozing while she went in to eat dinner with her parents. Later, she was helping clear away the plates when the phone rang in the hall.

Dawn rushed to answer it. It was Aunt Jenny, her mom's sister.

"Aunt Jenny! How's Tansy? Is she missing me? Have you taken her for lots of walks?" The pent-up questions spilled out of her. "She loves it in the park. Her favorite food is meaty chunks. And how's she getting along with Bella? Have they been playing together?" Bella was her aunt's gentle old Labrador.

"Whoa! Slow down, honey!" Dawn could tell her aunt was smiling. "Tansy's doing fine, although she's running circles around poor old Bella. We're giving her lots of extra cuddles. Don't worry about her," she said in her kind, sensible way.

"I'm trying not to, but I miss her so much," Dawn said sadly. She knew that she always would, but she had to try to be grown-up about this. Tansy had a good home with her aunt and Bella for company. "Can I come see her this weekend?"

"Come any time you like. It's always nice to see you," Aunt Jenny said warmly. "Tansy's still your dog, you know. She always will be." After they chatted for a few more minutes, they said their goodbyes and Dawn passed the phone to her mom.

Dawn had a lump in her throat. She swallowed hard, determined not to cry as she left her mom and aunt talking and wandered into the kitchen. Putting thoughts of Tansy aside, she opened the fridge and chose a carrot and some juicy lettuce leaves.

Stuffing the food under her top, Dawn went into her bedroom to see if Arrow was awake. The box on her bedside chest was empty.

"Arrow?" she whispered, looking around.

There was a faint scratching noise. A pink nose followed by a fluffy little head with pricked ears appeared from beneath the bed. "I have been exploring your territory," Arrow said, his nose twitching.

Dawn smiled. She'd never thought of her bedroom as "territory" before—but she supposed it was in a way! She sank down beside him and pulled out the food.

"Are you hungry? I don't know what magic bunnies eat, so I got you these."

"In Moonglow Meadow I eat juicy

grass and sweet wild flowers. This is strange food!" Arrow hopped forward and nudged the carrot, sniffing it curiously. He took a tiny nibble and then did the same with a lettuce leaf. "I like it!"

Dawn watched, smiling as he munched through the food and then groomed himself. When he'd finished, she lifted Arrow on to her bed and lay down with him sprawled out full length on her chest.

She cuddled his warm little body delightedly, enjoying the clean grassy scent of his fur. "I can't wait for you to meet Tansy. I'm going to see her this weekend. She belongs to me, but she's went to live with my Aunt Jenny and Bella," she explained.

"I would like to meet Tansy very much. What kind of rabbit is she?" Arrow asked, tucking his front paws beneath him.

Dawn laughed. "Tansy isn't a rabbit! She's a white-and-brown Jack Russell terrier."

"A dog?" Arrow blinked at her nervously. "I know of these, but we do not have any in Moonglow Meadow. Is Tansy friendly?"

"Oh yes. She wouldn't hurt a fly," Dawn assured him confidently, although she wasn't actually sure that her little dog had ever met a rabbit before. She was looking forward to all the fun Tansy and Arrow would have, running around her aunt's huge garden.

Chapter FOUR

The following morning Dawn woke to find something furry curled up right under her chin. It took a moment for her to realize that it was Arrow and he was trembling all over.

"Hey, what's wrong?" she whispered, stroking him gently.

The magic bunny sat up, blinking his big brown eyes. "I thought one of those giant noisy monsters that grumble outside was chasing me!"

Dawn frowned, listening hard, but there were only a few cars going past the apartment. That's what he meant! So many things in this big new world must seem strange and scary to the tiny bunny.

"Cars and buses aren't monsters. They're just things people travel around in. I used to be a bit scared of them when I was little. Don't worry, I won't let them hurt you. I'm very good at crossing the street," she reassured him.

Arrow had stopped trembling. "I must try to be braver," he decided.

"I think you're already a brave little bunny!" Dawn crooned. "It took a lot of courage to come here on this mission."

"Thank you, Dawn." He touched her

chin with the tip of his damp pink nose.

"You're welcome! I love having you for my friend. I really wish we could spend all day together." She made a face. "Unfortunately, I have to get ready for school instead. It's my second day in my new class."

"What is school?"

"It's where kids go to learn things," Dawn explained.

Arrow's cute face lit up with eagerness. "We do not have such things in

Moonglow Meadow. I will come with you!"

"I don't know if that's a good idea," Dawn said doubtfully, imagining the complications of having a bunny hopping around the classroom—even an invisible one. But then her tummy fluttered at the thought of being teased or laughed at again, and she decided it would be good to have her magical new friend with her.

"Well, maybe it would be all right," she said.

After a quick breakfast, Dawn and Arrow hurried to school. They made it to the playground as the bell was ringing for class. Dawn filed inside to the coatroom with everyone else.

Some kids she recognized from yesterday's class smiled at her. Dawn smiled back as she hung up her coat. She turned around, about to speak to them, but they were already walking away, chattering excitedly about the Easter celebrations. Everyone was so distracted with getting ready for Easter that Dawn thought she would never make friends!

Her smile faded as she unzipped her bag. She was really glad that Arrow was here.

The magic bunny had just popped his head out of the opening when a hand snatched her bag and whisked it away.

Arrow gave a startled cry.

"Hey! Don't! You'll hurt him!" Dawn cried without thinking. Whipping around, she saw Emma clutching the bag to her chest.

"Hurt who?" Emma asked. "Did you

bring your teddy bear to school?" she joked in a silly baby voice.

Dawn was too worried about Arrow to care what Emma thought. "Give me my bag! Now!" she demanded.

"Why don't I see what's in it first?" Emma teased, her eyes sparkling. "Do you have something yummy in your lunchbox? I've got some of Mom's lemon cake. Tell you what! I'll swap you some."

Dawn hesitated, puzzled. Emma almost seemed to be making some kind of effort now, but she was too terrified that Arrow was going to get squished to think any more about it. She lunged forward and tried to grab her bag back.

Emma danced away, holding it up out of reach. Dawn stood still, feeling helpless. She knew this game. It could go on for ages.

Suddenly, she felt a warm prickling sensation down her spine. Something very strange was about to happen.

Dawn saw a puff of crystal dust shoot up out of the bag's opening. The dust transformed into a big whoosh of what looked like thin brightly colored tentacles.

Pink, yellow, and blue, they made comical whizzing and burping noises as they shot out in all directions, forming a ragged clump and making a beeline for Emma.

Splat! Splop! Sploosh!

Emma's head, shoulders and the front of her school uniform were immediately covered in sticky party streamers.

"Aargh! Get it off me!" she cried in a panic, throwing up her arms in shock. Dawn's bag went sailing high into the air.

"Arrow!" Dawn almost tripped over her own feet as she tried to catch her bag.

Her fingers closed on thin air as the bag hovered out of reach for a moment and then floated away to land gently on a bench at the far side of the coatroom. Arrow hopped out with a flick of his fluffy tail and sat there looking innocent with rainbows dancing in his big brown eyes. He waved a front paw at Dawn to show he was fine.

"Phew!" Dawn's heartbeat slowly returned to normal.

Luckily, Emma hadn't noticed the floating bag. "Yuck! This stuff's gross!" she complained, going cross-eyed as she pulled bits of twirly pink stuff off the end of her nose.

Dawn felt laughter bubbling up in her. "I thought you liked jokes!" she spluttered. Emma didn't answer. She shook herself like a wet dog and the streamers tumbled on to the floor and started to dissolve.

Dawn went over to Arrow. She picked him up, tucked him under one arm and grabbed her bag before heading toward the door of the classroom. "Arrow! That was so naughty!" she scolded gently. "But maybe Emma will stop being such a pain with me now. Oops, sorry!" She only just managed to stop herself from knocking into Miss Walker, who was coming into the coatroom.

"Why aren't you two in class? What's going on?" the teacher asked.

"I . . . um . . . " Dawn didn't know quite what to say without getting in trouble, but she wasn't going to tattle.

Miss Walker seemed to have worked things out for herself. Frowning, she turned to Emma. "Look at you covered in a mess. I bet you've been playing silly tricks again. I'm very disappointed in you. I expected you to make Dawn feel welcome and help her get settled in class."

"I was only playing with her bag as a joke!" Emma argued, looking at Dawn with a wounded expression. "It was meant to be funny."

"Jokes aren't funny if no one's laughing, Emma," the teacher said firmly. "Now I want you both in class. Pronto!"

Hanging her head, Emma went to the classroom. Dawn walked beside her, no longer feeling like laughing. Why did she have the feeling that this time what happened hadn't been all Emma's fault?

She sighed. It looked like it was going to be another long school day, sitting next to each other without speaking.

Chapter FIVE

"I don't know what I'd do without you in class!" Dawn whispered to Arrow on Saturday morning. They were in the supermarket with her mom. "Since Miss Walker told us about the Easter Fair everyone's too busy to be friends. And Emma's always with Alesha and Vicky. She probably hates me after she got into trouble with Miss Walker in the coatroom."

Arrow was sitting with his front legs looped over the opening of her shoulder bag. He looked up at her. "Perhaps she would like it if you talked to her. I do not think that Emma is a mean person," he said wisely.

Dawn fell silent as she wondered whether Arrow could be right. But even if she wanted to make things up with

Emma, she didn't know how to start.

She quickly forgot about Emma when she noticed Arrow licking his lips at a display of particularly juicy carrots. Reaching for a bag, she filled it right up. Mrs. Kenton raised her eyebrows as Dawn dumped the carrots in the shopping cart.

"Are you sure you're feeling all right?"

"Yep! I *love* carrots! But that doesn't mean I don't want any Easter eggs!" Dawn added hastily. She was a big fan of chocolate.

Her mom laughed. "I think I'm finished. Let's go. You must be looking forward to seeing Tansy." They were going to Aunt Jenny's house straight after the supermarket.

"You bet!" Dawn exclaimed. "Can we stop into the pet store on the way please?

I want to get a present for Tansy." *And something for Arrow*, she thought.

Her mom nodded. "No problem. I'll park outside and wait for you in the car."

In the store, Dawn counted out her spending money. There was just enough for a dog biscuit shaped like a bone and a rabbit chew made from parsley and wheat. Before going back to the car, Dawn hid the rabbit treat in her pocket so her mom wouldn't be suspicious.

A few minutes later, they drove up to her aunt's front drive and her mom climbed out. "We're here," Dawn whispered excitedly to Arrow, who was standing on his back legs and peering out the side window. "I can't wait for you to meet Tansy."

Her aunt appeared at the garden gate.

Bella, her elderly Labrador, was at her side and she had a little brown-and-white dog in her arms.

"Hi, Aunt Jenny! Bella! Tansy!" Dawn called, waving as she opened the car door. She glanced quickly over her shoulder at Arrow. "I think you should jump into my bag—" she began to say.

All of a sudden Tansy wriggled free from Aunt Jenny. Yapping excitedly, she exploded out the front gate, bounding straight into the car and into Dawn's lap.

Arrow's muffled squeal of panic was lost in a torrent of barking and tail wagging. The magic bunny hastily leaped under the front seat.

"Hi, girl! Have you missed me?" Dawn grabbed Tansy's collar as the little dog licked her chin and the end of her nose.

"Hey! I took a shower today! Calm down. There's someone I want you to meet!"

Tansy's nose twitched. She stiffened as she seemed to catch Arrow's scent.

Wroof! An eager whine rumbled in her throat as she struggled to get free again.

"Be gentle!" Dawn scolded, hanging on tight. "It's okay, Arrow. Tansy's just excited. She won't hurt . . . Oh!"

Grrr-uuf! Tansy had slipped her collar. She peered down under the front seat, her mouth lolling open in a doggy grin as she prepared to jump at the magic bunny.

Arrow had other ideas. He shot out of the car and streaked around the side of the house. Tansy gave chase, barking with excitement.

"Oh my gosh!" Dawn almost fell onto the pavement as she scrambled after them.

Aunt Jenny and Mrs. Kenton watched openmouthed as Arrow, Tansy, and then Dawn rushed past them.

"Wherever did that little white rabbit come from?" Aunt Jenny exclaimed.

Oh no! Dawn realized that Arrow

must have forgotten to stay invisible! She pounded down the garden path, just in time to see him leap into a bush at the bottom.

Tansy wasn't far behind Arrow. She skidded to a halt, tail wagging. With a triumphant bark, she plunged in headfirst after him.

Dawn saw something golden glow in the depth of the bush. The magic key! She felt the familiar warm tingling sensation down her spine as a tall column of shimmering crystal dust rose from the bush. There was a rustle of frantic movement, followed by a surprised bark.

Yipe! Tansy shot upward out of the bush like a cork from a bottle.

The little Jack Russell landed on top of a very small birdhouse that was hanging

from a tree overhead. Tansy perched there, balancing on the tips of all four paws. Flattening her ears, she whined nervously as she looked down at the lawn.

Dawn couldn't help smiling at her mournful expression. "I warned you about being too rough! Arrow's a very special little rabbit!"

Arrow hopped out from under the bush. He looked up at Tansy indignantly, dusting himself down with his fluffy front paws.

"I'm sorry, Arrow. I should have warned you that Tansy gets overexcited. Are you okay?"

The magic bunny nodded. "I am fine now."

"Good. So how about you two make friends?" she whispered as she heard her mom, her aunt, and Bella approaching. "Tansy needs to get down from there. And I think you need to become invisible."

The key around Arrow's neck glowed brightly and a final cloud of sparkling crystal dust surrounded Tansy, carrying her gently down onto the lawn. Arrow hopped up to the little dog, touched his nose to hers, and then sprang away. Wagging her tail, Tansy padded carefully after Arrow.

Dawn breathed. "Phew! Panic over!"

"Where did that little white rabbit go?" Dawn's mom asked as she approached.

"Um . . . it ran off. I think it was a wild one . . ." Dawn replied.

Aunt Jenny nodded. "You're probably right. Look at Tansy, showing off in front of you. She was having a lovely game of chase all by herself. It's a shame that Bella's too old to run around with her."

Dawn grinned as she watched Tansy and Arrow playing their secret game. She spent a happy hour playing with them both before enjoying a delicious picnic

of sandwiches and yummy homemade chocolate cake. Before leaving, Dawn gave Tansy the bone-shaped biscuit. She immediately settled down with it between her front paws, gnawing it happily.

Dawn tried not to feel too sad as they headed back. Tansy was obviously well cared for, but the visit had reminded her how much she missed her little dog.

"I wish I could have brought her back

with us," she whispered to Arrow, who was nibbling his rabbit chew.

Her fluffy friend stopped munching long enough to rub his soft cheek against her hand. "I hope that Tansy will be able to live with you again one day."

"Me too." Dawn sighed. At least she had Arrow as a friend. She felt herself cheering up as she stroked him.

Chapter SIX

It was Friday, the day before the Easter Fair. In the school hall, kids were busily pinning up a banner that read "Pets' Corner: prizes for the best kept pet." Others were blowing up balloons, organizing stalls with games, and arranging things for sale.

Dawn stood with a group of kids, waiting to be given a job. She was

holding Arrow's invisible little body in the crook of one arm, over which she'd looped her school jacket.

Arrow craned his neck, watching all the activity with interest. "What is this for?"

"It's called Easter," Dawn whispered after quickly checking that no one was watching her. "People go to church and have parties and eat lots of special food like chocolate eggs and cupcakes decorated with fluffy chicks and bunnies. Not real ones," she said, trying not to smile as Arrow's eyes widened in alarm.

Nearby, Miss Walker was giving

out more jobs. "The barrel needs to be filled with shredded paper for the Grab Bag . . ."

Suddenly, there was a loud bang as a balloon burst.

Everyone laughed, but poor Arrow almost jumped out of his fur. His ears flattened in terror and he leaped to the floor. He darted behind a wooden stand that was leaning against a wall and crouched there trembling.

"And if someone would like to put that notice stand together, please," Miss Walker was saying. "It needs to go outside the door and—"

"I'll do it!" Dawn was across the room in an instant and bending down to scoop the scared little bunny into her arms. His tiny heart was fluttering against her hand.

"It's okay, Arrow," she whispered. "I know it was a very loud noise, but silly old bursting balloons can't hurt you."

"I will not be frightened by such loud noises again," Arrow announced proudly.

"Good for you." Dawn tried not to smile too much. She had her back to everyone, so she risked a quick cuddle as she carried him to a nearby bookcase and put him gently on the top. "There you go. No one will step on you now."

Arrow's eyes lit up as he spotted a spider plant and immediately began nibbling one of the leaves.

"Hey, leave that alone!" Dawn said. It could be very awkward to explain what was happening if someone noticed the plant's leaves gradually disappearing.

"Charming!" said a familiar voice.

Dawn whipped around in surprise, realizing that she'd spoken more loudly than she'd intended to. Emma was there and had obviously assumed Dawn was talking to her.

"I only came over to help you with that wooden sign thing," Emma said huffily.

"I wasn't talking to . . . I didn't mean . . ." Dawn spread her hands helplessly as she knew she couldn't explain about Arrow.

"Don't bother!" Emma stormed off to help with the Grab Bag.

Dawn watched her go in disbelief. After this, Emma would never want to be friends with her.

After breakfast on Saturday morning, Dawn called her aunt to check on Tansy. Her aunt held the phone close to Tansy, so the little dog could hear Dawn's voice. "Be good for Aunt Jenny, Tansy! Love you lots." Dawn made kissing noises into the phone and felt the usual tug of sadness as she heard Tansy's soft little whine. She could hardly bear to wait another week until she saw her again.

"Everything okay, honey?" her dad asked, squeezing Dawn's shoulder gently as she hung up the phone.

Dawn nodded.

"You need cheering up. Come on. Let's go to the Easter Fair. I'm looking forward to seeing your classroom and meeting some of your new friends." He jingled the car keys and went toward the open front door. "Your mom's already in the car."

"I'll be right there!" Dawn raced to her room to get Arrow, who was just finishing his breakfast carrot.

At the school they joined the other kids and their parents filing into the classrooms for the Easter Fair. The hall was bustling with people enjoying themselves. Older children from the school band were on the stage playing their instruments. Dawn grinned as two little girls from the kindergarten class made cheeky faces at her. Their faces were painted to look like cute Easter bunnies and they wore headbands with long pink ears!

Miss Walker came over to greet them. "Hi, Dawn. Hello, Mr. and Mrs. Kenton. Glad you could make it."

"Hi, Miss Walker," Dawn said. "It looks great in here."

"Yes, it does. Everyone's worked really hard to get things ready. Including you," she said warmly. "Dawn, would you like to sell some raffle tickets while I have a quick word with your mom and dad?"

Dawn took a bundle of tickets and she and Arrow set off down the hall.

Dawn wandered about, selling tickets as she went. Inside her shoulder bag, Arrow stretched up on his haunches so he could look out. His little pink nose twitched at all the exciting smells.

Over at Pets' Corner, Emma was holding a large glossy black rabbit in her arms. The judge presented her with a shiny gold ribbon. "First prize goes to Emma Packard's beautiful rabbit, Blackberry!"

"Yay!" Emma kissed her rabbit's head. "We won! Good job, Blackberry."

Arrow spotted the big black rabbit and Dawn felt him stiffen inside her bag. "My enemies have found me!"

"What? Where?" Dawn spun around and clutched her bag protectively. "Oh, you mean Emma's rabbit. That's not—"

She was too late. In a single mighty leap, Arrow landed on the floor and dashed under the nearest table.

"Oh no!" Dawn shot into action. Hastily thrusting a handful of coins and raffle tickets into her jeans pocket, she threw herself to her knees and scuttled under the table after her friend. "Arrow, wait!"

Arrow didn't notice. In his desperation

to escape his fierce enemies he raced about blindly. Dawn lost sight of him and crawled out from under a table to look around the hall.

There he was! Somehow he'd ended up right back near Emma, who had just put Blackberry back into his carrier. Dawn saw Emma's eyes widen as she spotted the terrified little bunny. Bending down, she picked him up.

With a sinking heart, Dawn realized that Arrow was so scared that he'd forgotten to stay invisible again—just like when Tansy had chased him!

"Hello. Aren't you gorgeous? I'm sure no one brought a little white bunny here today. You must be lost." Emma was cradling Arrow gently in her arms. "Do you want to come home with me? You can be a friend for Blackberry."

Dawn froze. *Now* what was she going to do?

Chapter SEVEN

Dawn spoke without thinking. "That bunny's mine!" she blurted out as she raced toward Emma.

"Excuse me? I don't think so. Where's its carrier then? Anyway, I saw it first and I'm keeping it." Emma held Arrow gently but firmly, a determined look on her face.

"Arrow's a him. Just give him to me, Emma!"

Dawn bit her lip. She knew Arrow couldn't use his magic to save himself with so many people around. It was up to her to sort this out somehow.

A few kids had wandered over to admire the fluffy white bunny. Other heads were turning to look at them.

Dawn tried to calm down and reason with Emma. "Look, I can't explain. But it's *really* important that you give him to me," she said desperately.

Emma frowned. "Why? Oh, I get it. You think I won't take care of him properly!"

"No. Of course you would. Blackberry's well taken care of. It's not that . . ." Dawn's mind seemed to have gone blank. How could she explain without giving away Arrow's secret? To make things worse, she saw her parents coming over. *Oh, great*, she groaned inwardly.

"Dawn? What's going on?" her mom asked.

Dawn took a deep breath. "It's this cute little white rabbit. He needs a home."

Her mom looked closely at Arrow. "How odd. It looks just like the one Tansy was chasing the other day at Aunt Jenny's."

Dawn shook her head firmly. "No. That

was definitely a wild one, remember? So can I have him? Please, Mom? Dad? He'd hardly take up any room. I'll do anything—laundry, ironing. I'll even wash the car for a whole month and you don't have to pay me . . ."

"Huh?" Emma frowned. "I thought you said he was already yours?"

Dawn didn't answer. Luckily, no one was paying any attention to Emma.

She crossed her finger and toes and squeezed her eyes shut. Please, please let Mom and Dad say yes!

"I'm sorry, honey," her mom said gently. "You know the rules about pets."

"Your mom's right," her dad said. "But I know how much you miss Tansy. Maybe we could get you a goldfish."

Dawn's spirits sank. She didn't want a

goldfish, she wanted Arrow back! There was nothing she could do but watch Emma open Blackberry's pet carrier, slip Arrow inside and close the door.

Arrow seemed to have realized that Blackberry wasn't one of the fierce dark rabbits from his homeland, but his brown eyes still pleaded with Dawn through the wire mesh side. "Do I have to go home

with Emma? I want to stay with you."

Dawn felt her heart turn over as she bent close to whisper so that only he could hear. "I know. I want that too. Don't worry! I'll think of some way of getting you back. Promise."

"Gotta go!" Emma sang out, picking up the carrier. "Mom and Dad are waiting for me in the parking lot." She stalked toward the open door and went outside.

Dawn swallowed angry tears. Despite her promise to Arrow, she didn't see how she was going to get him back.

There's no way I'm giving up! I have to do something, she told herself firmly.

As Dawn struggled to think of a plan, something shiny on the hall floor caught her eye.

Arrow's magic key!

It must have come off when Emma picked him up. Moonglow Meadow needed the key's magic to stay lush and green. She had to get it back to him!

Dawn raced outside. "I'll be right back!" she called over her shoulder to her parents.

In her haste, Dawn rolled over onto the side of her foot and a hot pain shot through her ankle. Trying to ignore it, she frantically scanned the rows of parked cars. There! She spotted Emma putting the pet carrier in the back of a red car.

"Wait! I have to talk to you!" Dawn cried, half running and half limping over.

Emma straightened and looked at her in surprise.

Dawn saw that Emma's parents were talking to people a few feet away. It was now or never. Inside the car, Arrow's little face was pressed hopefully against the wire mesh.

"Emma, please listen," Dawn puffed. "This is going to sound totally weird, but it's the truth. I swear."

Emma folded her arms. "Okay, go on."

"I couldn't tell you this in there, but that little white bunny really is mine," Dawn rushed on. "I smuggled Arrow into my bedroom and he lives there. Mom and Dad would go crazy if they knew. No pets are allowed in Redford Mansions . . ."

"Redford Mansions? Is that where you live?" Emma interrupted.

"Yes. We just moved into one of the apartments," Dawn continued, eager to get Arrow back. "I brought Arrow here in my shoulder bag, but he got scared by something and jumped out. I was just about to put him back in my bag when you picked him up."

Emma blinked at her, obviously not sure whether to believe what she was saying. Then her lips curved in a smile. "Wow! That's so cool. I thought you were so boring. You hardly say a word to anybody in class—especially me."

"I can be kind of shy with new people, and everybody's been so busy," Dawn admitted, blushing. "And . . . and I don't like being teased."

"Yeah, well. I can be shy sometimes, too."

Dawn's jaw nearly dropped. Emma? Shy?

"People don't notice because I cover it up by making jokes and stuff. Maybe I go too far sometimes," Emma admitted. "I'm sorry." Suddenly, she seemed to make up her mind. "Okay. You can have Arrow back, but you have to promise me something."

Dawn frowned suspiciously. "What?"

"You'll bring him to visit me and Blackberry sometimes."

Inside the carrier, the glossy black rabbit

was licking Arrow's ears, while the magic bunny's eyes were closed in contentment.

Dawn laughed. "Okay. Deal!"

Emma reached into the car, unfastened the carrier, and lifted out Arrow. "You'd better put him in your bag before your mom and dad see him. They're coming out of the school," she said, glancing over Dawn's shoulder.

"Okay. Thanks." Dawn opened her bag. "Quickly, Arrow!" Her fluffy white friend gave a mighty leap out of Emma's arms and dived straight inside.

Emma grinned, impressed. "That was some jump! Anyone would think Arrow understood what you said!"

Dawn smiled back. *If only you knew*, she thought.

"See you on Monday!" Emma said.

"See you! And thanks again." Dawn tried not to limp as she walked away.

Arrow leaned up out of her bag, so that she could slip the golden chain around his neck. "Thank you for rescuing me and returning my key! You are a very good friend, Dawn."

"I just couldn't bear the thought of losing you. Oh!" Dawn gritted her teeth and stumbled as pain zinged up her leg. Her ankle was throbbing horribly.

Arrow's furry brow crinkled in concern. "You are hurt! I will help you."

Dawn felt a warm tingling sensation down her spine as Arrow's key started pulsing with light. Arrow twitched his little pink nose and a cloud of crystal dust appeared, shimmering with a thousand tiny rainbows. To Dawn's amazement, the magical dust swirled around her sore ankle for a few seconds, before seeming

to sink into it. Her ankle turned icy cold before suddenly feeling fine—no pain at all.

"Wow! Thanks, Arrow. I'm fine now. Come on. Let's go and find Mom and Dad and get you home!"

Chapter EIGHT

Later that night, Arrow sat on Dawn's bedroom windowsill as they both looked out at the starry sky. The moon was spreading pale light on the street below.

It had been a long and exciting day. Dawn bit back a yawn as she wondered if the same moon shone down on Moonglow Meadow.

Suddenly, Dawn felt Arrow stiffen beside her. "Look there!" Arrow pointed with a front paw as a group of black shapes crossed a pool of streetlight on the opposite side of the road. "Dark rabbits! My enemies are close," he said in a panicky voice.

Dawn quickly snatched him up and drew the curtains closed with her free hand. She could feel him trembling. "I don't think they saw you. And you're safe in here with me."

Arrow leaned forward to peep out a tiny crack in the curtains. "The dark rabbits are moving away," he said with relief.

Dawn hugged Arrow protectively until he calmed down. She put him on her bed.

Almost at once, the magic key began flashing more brightly than Dawn had ever seen it.

"Moonglow Meadow will soon be in need of more magic!" Arrow exclaimed.

Dawn gasped. "Do you have to leave right now?" she asked anxiously.

"No. Not until the key glows constantly. But then I may have to leave at once without saying good-bye."

Dawn bit back her sadness. "Will . . . will you be coming back to live with me again?"

Arrow looked up at her with gentle soft brown eyes. "I am afraid that is not possible. Once I leave here, the magic trail to this place will be closed forever. I am sorry. I hope you understand, Dawn."

Dawn nodded sadly. She tried not to think about Arrow leaving, especially after almost losing him once already today. She decided to enjoy every single moment of the time they had left together.

The following afternoon, Dawn and Arrow were sitting on the grass in a quiet corner of the grounds that surrounded Redford Mansions. Dawn munched on a chocolate Easter egg as she watched him investigating a patch of weeds. After she finished the egg, she squeezed the shiny wrapper into a tight ball.

"Hey, Arrow! Want to learn how to play fetch?" She rolled the ball toward him.

Arrow's ears swiveled. He looked up and then hopped forward and grasped the ball in his mouth.

"That's it," Dawn encouraged. "Bring it to me and I'll throw for you again."

Arrow soon got the idea. They played fetch for a while until, at last, he flopped down, panting. "That was fun!"

Dawn picked him up. "Let's go inside and you can take a nap."

The phone rang in the hall as they came in.

"I bet that's Aunt Jenny!" Dawn exclaimed eagerly as she answered it. "Hi, Aunt Jen! Oh—" She paused in surprise as she realized who it was. "Emma?"

"Hi, Dawn. I wondered if you and Arrow would like to come to my house for lunch tomorrow? Mom says it's okay."

"Um . . . I guess I could," Dawn said, feeling unsure. She still wasn't quite used to this new friendly Emma.

"You don't have to, if you don't want to," Emma said quietly.

Dawn made up her mind. "I'd love to!"

"Great! This is where I live . . ."

"I'm glad that you're starting to make some new friends, honey," Mr. Kenton said as he dropped Dawn and Arrow off at Emma's.

"Me too," Dawn said.

The house was at the end of the street. There were pots of bright flowers on either side of a cheerful red front door. Dawn rang the bell. After a little while, when no one had appeared, she rang it again.

"I don't think anyone's in here. I knew it! This is another of Emma's silly jokes!" She sighed. "I bet she's been waiting all this time to pay me back for covering her in those sticky streamers in the coatroom!"

A slight breeze stirred Arrow's fluffy white fur. He seemed disappointed. "I was looking forward to seeing Blackberry again. He is a fine rabbit."

"That's it. We're leaving!" Dawn was turning away when the door opened.

"Sorry! I only just heard the bell," Emma said brightly. "We were all in the garden. Come in."

Dawn calmed down as she followed Emma into the house. She'd been totally wrong about her this time.

Emma's mom greeted Dawn with a warm smile. Delicious cooking smells wafted out of the kitchen behind her. "Hello, Dawn. This must be the little lost white bunny you've adopted."

"Hi, Mrs. Packard," Dawn said politely. "Yes. His name is Arrow."

"Why don't you show Dawn and Arrow where Blackberry lives, Emma? I'll call you when lunch is ready."

Emma led the way outside to a garden shed and opened the door. "Ta-da!"

"Wow! This is bunny heaven!" Dawn said, admiring the cage, neat shelves, and sturdy bunny run that was scattered with toys. There were clean dishes, packets of rabbit food, and bags of straw on shelves. The shed smelled of sweet hay.

Arrow's pink nose was twitching in

approval. "This is a good place."

"I forgot how sweet Arrow is. Can I hold him?" Emma asked.

Arrow didn't seem to mind so Dawn handed him over.

"Hi, Arrow," Emma crooned, stroking him gently. "He has the most unusual eyes. They're like caramel candy speckled with rainbow dust."

"Arrow's one of a kind," Dawn agreed.

"You can cuddle Blackberry, if you like." Emma opened the cage, so Dawn could lift him out. "I brushed him for a while so his coat is all shiny," she said proudly.

At Emma's suggestion, they put the bunnies into the run. After some friendly nose twitching and fur snuffling, Arrow and Blackberry began rooting through the

straw and chewing toys.

"Look at that. Instant best friends!" Emma grinned, her eyes sparkling. "I love animals." She began talking about all the pets she'd had. ". . . and a gerbil and two rats. And I used to have a cute Yorkshire terrier called Maisie. How about you?"

Dawn chewed at her lip. "I . . . I have a dog called Tansy. But she doesn't live with me anymore." To her surprise, once she started, it was easy to tell Emma everything. When she finished she was biting back tears.

Emma listened in silence until Dawn had finished. "Oh, poor you. That's so awful," she sympathized. "I'd hate it if I had to give up Blackberry." A look of determination came over her face. "Your apartment is in Redford Mansions, right? There might be something we can do about Tansy. Leave it to me."

Chapter NINE

"It was fun at Emma's house today, wasn't it?" Dawn said to Arrow. After a delicious lunch of sandwiches and Mrs. Packard's amazing lemon cake, Emma's dad had driven them back to Redford Mansions.

"I had a good time, too," Arrow said as the elevator door pinged open at their floor.

"It was nice of her to say she'd try to do something about Tansy, but I don't think anybody can."

Arrow looked up at her. "Emma seems to be a person who is true to her word."

Dawn stroked the tiny rabbit fondly. "Well, I do appreciate her wanting to help," she agreed.

Dawn walked into the apartment and found her mom in the hall. She had her coat on and looked worried. "Mom? Is something wrong?"

Mrs. Kenton nodded. "I'm afraid Aunt Jenny's just phoned. It's Tansy. She's escaped somehow and run away."

Dawn gasped. "Oh no!"

Mrs. Kenton grabbed her coat. "Come on! We're going straight over to help look for her!"

Dawn's heart was in her mouth as they drove across town. She sat in silence, cuddling Arrow.

Aunt Jenny was apologetic. "I'm so sorry, Dawn. Tansy must have slipped out when my back was turned. We've searched everywhere, but there's no sign of her. I'm about to call the vet . . ."

Dawn knew what that meant. She tried not to think about busy roads and other dangers. "Where could she be? I don't know where to look," she whispered to Arrow.

"I will help you!" His magical key glowed as he pointed a little white paw at the ground. A fountain of crystal dust whooshed out, revealing a trail of glowing doggy footprints that led up the road and disappeared around the corner. "This way, Dawn!"

"Yay!" Dawn cheered, hastily turning it into a cough as her mom and Aunt Jenny turned to look at her in surprise. "I've got a hunch about where Tansy went!"

Dawn ran after Arrow, who was running away, his white bobtail flashing. She raced along, following the trail of glowing doggy footprints. As she turned a corner, she glimpsed Arrow's tiny form passing some stores along the high street.

This was where she and mom had gone shopping. Somehow Tansy must have picked up Dawn's trail. Arrow was following the shining paw prints that seemed to be going in the direction of Redford Mansions.

Dawn felt renewed hope as she ran faster. She was only seconds behind Arrow when she raced into the apartment's gardens.

"What's that on the bench?" Dawn narrowed her eyes. "It's not . . . It can't be! Tansy?" She gasped.

"Yes, Dawn. She is safe."

Something in Arrow's voice made Dawn look at him.

His magic key was glowing constantly like a miniature gold star. The moment Dawn had been dreading was here. A cloud of shimmering crystal dust appeared, swirling around Arrow and twinkling with rainbow sparkles.

Suddenly, Arrow appeared in his true form. A tiny fluffy white bunny no longer, but a majestic rabbit the size of a large cat. His silky pure-white fur was flecked with silver and his large ears had glittering silver tips.

"Arrow!" Dawn gasped. She had almost forgotten how beautiful he was. "Are you leaving right now?"

Sadness flickered across his chocolate-brown eyes for a moment. "I must. Moonglow Meadow urgently needs more of the key's magic."

Dawn's eyes stung with tears. She bit them back as she knew she must be brave and allow her friend to go. She bent down and threw her arms around the handsome white rabbit and laid her cheek against his silky fur.

"I'll never forget you," she whispered sadly.

"I will not forget you, either." Arrow allowed her to hug him one last time and then moved gently away. "Farewell. And always follow your dreams, Dawn," he said in a velvety voice.

There was a final flash of light, and crystal dust rained down around Dawn, tinkling softly as it hit the ground. Arrow faded and was gone.

Dawn stood there, stunned by how fast everything had happened. Her chest ached with the effort of holding back tears. Something lay on the grass. It was a single rainbow crystal drop. Bending down, she picked it up. The drop tingled against her palm as it turned into a tiny pure-white pebble in the shape of a bunny.

Dawn slipped it into her pocket. She knew she would always keep it as a reminder of the magic bunny and the wonderful adventure they had shared.

As she straightened up, Tansy rushed over, whining and wagging her tail. Dawn picked her up. "Hello, girl! You're safe with me now."

"Dawn!"

Dawn turned around to see Emma running toward her. "I've got some amazing news! Is this Tansy?"

Dawn blinked in puzzlement. "Emma? What news? When did you get here?"

"My dad works for the company that owns Redford Mansions. He got special permission for you to have Tansy live with you! I couldn't wait to tell you, so I got Dad to give me a ride over here."

"That's incredible!" Dawn didn't know whether to laugh or cry. She knew that

Arrow would be watching with approval.

Take care. Wherever you are. And look after Moonglow Meadow, she whispered under her breath.

And then she smiled at her new best friend, Emma. "What I really need is someone who'll help take Tansy for walks. Any ideas?"

Emma smiled back. "You bet!"

About the AUTHOR

Sue Bentley's books for children often include animals, fairies, and magic. She lives in Northampton, England, in a house surrounded by a hedge so she can pretend she's in the middle of the countryside. She loves reading and going to the movies, and writes while watching the birds on the feeders outside her window and eating chocolate. Sue grew up surrounded by small animals and loved them all—especially her gentle pet rabbits whose fur smelled so sweetly of rain and grass.

Don't miss

Magic Bunny: Vacation Dreams

Magic Bunny: A Splash of Magic

Don't miss these
Magic Puppy books!

Don't miss these
Magic Kitten books!

Don't miss these
Magic Ponies books!

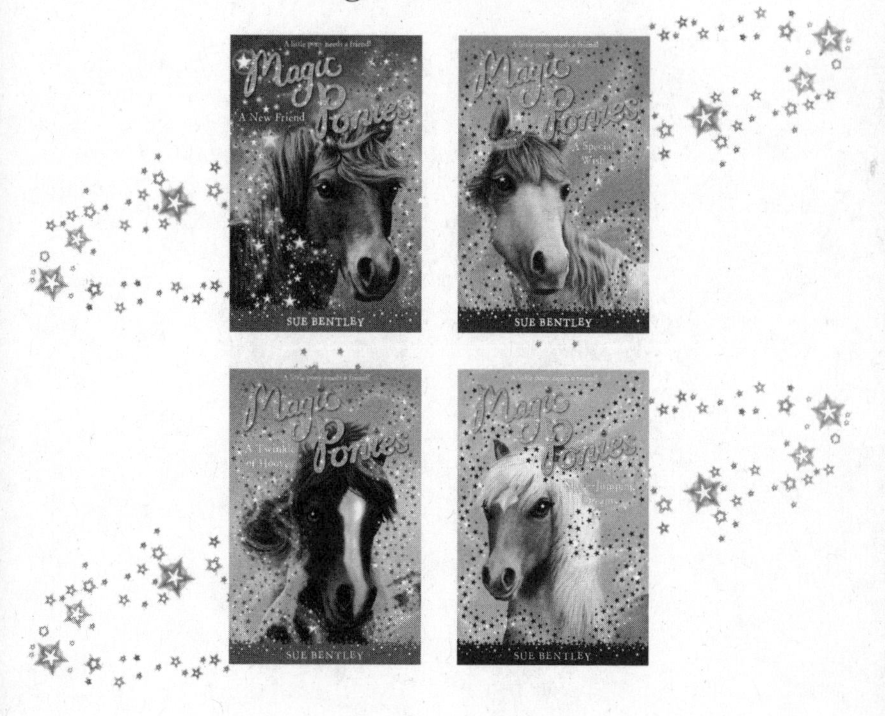